Francine the Superstar

A Marc Brown ARTHUR Chapter Book

Francine the Superstar

Text by Stephen Krensky

Based on a teleplay by Joe Fallon

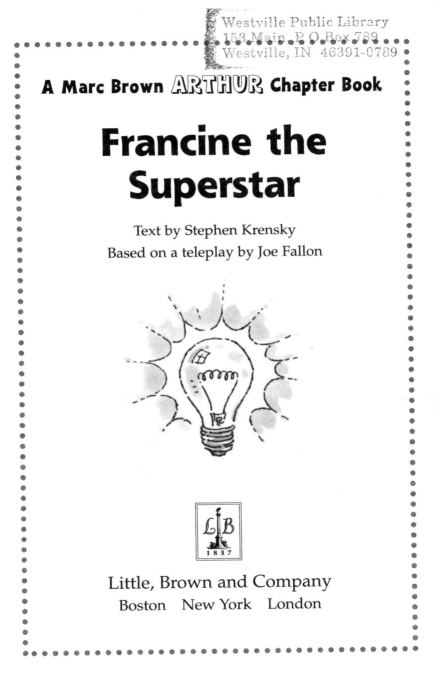

LB
1837

Little, Brown and Company
Boston   New York   London

First Edition

The characters and events portrayed in this book are fictitious. Any
similarity to real persons, living or dead, is coincidental and not intended
by the author.

Text has been reviewed and assigned a reading level by Laurel S. Ernst,
M.A., Teachers College, Columbia University, New York, New York;
reading specialist, Chappaqua, New York

Library of Congress Cataloging-in-Publication Data

Krensky, Stephen.
    Francine the superstar / text by Stephen Krensky ; based on a teleplay
by Joe Fallon — 1st ed.
        p. cm. — (A Marc Brown Arthur chapter book ; 22)
    Summary: After her friends help her get the lead in the third grade
play, Francine becomes so intent on making the play perfect that she
almost ruins it.
    ISBN 0-316-12227-0 (hc) — ISBN 0-316-12250-5 (pb)
    [1. Plays — Fiction. 2. Schools — Fiction. 3. Behavior — Fiction.]
I. Title.

PZ7.K883 Fr 2000
[Fic] — dc21   00-020701

10 9 8 7 6 5 4 3 2 1

WOR (hc)
COM-MO (pb)

Printed in the United States of America

For Steven and Helen Kellogg

Chapter 1

• • • • • • • • • • •

"Class, I have some important news," Mr. Ratburn announced one morning.

His third graders all looked up.

"Maybe he's canceling homework for the rest of the year," whispered Buster.

"Maybe he's canceling school for the rest of the year!" Binky added hopefully.

"I don't want to keep you in suspense about this," Mr. Ratburn went on. "It's our turn to put on a class play."

Francine started to worry. She had never had good luck with school plays. Once she had been the cherry tree in a play about George Washington, and Buster had chop-

1

ped her down. Another time she had portrayed Sir Isaac Newton sitting under an apple tree. An apple was supposed to drop on her head and make her discover gravity. Instead, the apple, a bucket, a ladder, and Arthur had fallen down and landed on her.

"Does anyone have any ideas for the subject?" Mr. Ratburn asked. "Keep in mind, we are doing a unit on inventors."

Sue Ellen raised her hand. "How about a spooky story about a mad scientist? There could be thunder and lightning and a huge monster" — everyone turned to listen — "who gets his arms pulled off!"

Binky jumped up, clapping. "Count me in!" he exclaimed. "And I want to do the pulling."

"Settle down, Binky," Mr. Ratburn cautioned him. "Imaginative, Sue Ellen, but a few too many special effects for us, I'm afraid. Anyone else? Yes, Alan?"

"Let's take a journey through space. We could build a giant spaceship. And I could manufacture the simulated rocket fuel."

Mr. Ratburn nodded. "I'm sure you could, but we might not have enough time to explore the galaxy."

Fern raised her hand. "Did you have something in mind, Mr. Ratburn?" she asked.

"Well, yes, as a matter of fact, I did." He paused. "What about the story of the great inventor Thomas Edison?"

"Did he invent anything that could fall on me?" asked Francine.

"No, no," Mr. Ratburn assured her. "You'd be perfectly safe. Can anyone name his inventions?"

Muffy raised her hand. "The Dewey decimal system?" she guessed.

"No, Muffy, Mr. Dewey did that. But Edison has received credit for inventing more things than anyone else in American history."

"Did he invent any sports?" asked Binky.

"I'm afraid not," said Mr. Ratburn. "But many of his inventions had great impact on everyday life. For example, he came up with the phonograph."

The students looked at him blankly.

"The record player," Mr. Ratburn continued. "It was before CDs. It played music with a needle."

"Ouch!" said Muffy, who couldn't think of needles without thinking of shots.

"You're kidding, right?" said Binky.

"No, I'm not. Edison also invented the lightbulb and the motion-picture camera."

"What about the computer?" asked Buster. "Or video games?"

"No, no, Edison lived a bit before that. Apparently, you could all benefit from exposure to a little more history. I think this play will be very educational for everyone. And it will also be a special opportunity for you to perform in front of a large audience."

Francine swallowed nervously. She had a bad feeling about this. If only Edison had invented the first aid kit, she would have felt much better.

Chapter 2

● ● ● ● ● ● ● ● ● ● ● ●

Inside the school auditorium, Mr. Ratburn stood on the stage with a clipboard. He was getting ready to start the auditions.

Arthur sneaked up behind him. "*Pssst!* Mr. Ratburn."

"What is it, Arthur?"

"I know you're about to assign the roles for the play. Could you please give Francine a good part? She's never had much luck in plays, and I know it would mean a lot to her."

"I'll certainly consider that, Arthur. Thank you."

As Arthur walked away, Muffy took his

place. "You must be feeling a lot of pressure, Mr. Ratburn."

"Oh, why is that?"

"Well, trying to match up the right actors with the right roles is hard work. And you don't even have any assistants to carry around those bottles of water for you."

"Life in the theater is often a challenge," Mr. Ratburn admitted. "I'm just doing the best I can."

Muffy nodded. "That's what I want to talk to you about. I think your job would be much easier if you could get one of the major parts settled. That's why I want to recommend Francine for something big. I'll bet she would be really good if she didn't get hit in the head with, you know, people or scenery or anything."

"I'll keep that in mind."

She darted away as Buster came up.

"Mr. Ratburn . . . ," he began.

His teacher held up a hand. "Before you say anything, Buster, let me guess. You realize what a big responsibility it is for me to be in charge of this play."

"Yes . . ."

"And you'd like to make things easier for me."

"Um, yes again."

"And so you wish to point out what a fine actress Francine is and how well suited she would be to a major role."

"Well, um, that's true."

"Excellent. Consider it said. You may go now."

Buster walked back to Arthur. "He's so smart, it's scary."

The kids were lined up on stage at the end of the auditions. Binky was finishing up.

"I was the wall in *Humpty Dumpty*," he explained. "Oh, and I was Plymouth Rock on Thanksgiving." He stuck out his arms and clenched his fists. "I hope there's a wall in this play, too, because I'm real steady."

Mr. Ratburn stepped forward. "Thank you, Binky." He called for the others to gather around. "All of your auditions were excellent, and it's time to make my selections. First, Buster . . ."

Buster jumped forward.

"Since you have so much energy, you'll be the first lightbulb. Arthur, you'll be the first phonograph. And Binky, you'll be a locomotive."

"Wow!" said Binky. "I didn't know Edison invented locomotives."

"He didn't. But you were born to play the part."

Binky raised his arms. "Yes!"

Mr. Ratburn handed out the other parts, leaving Francine standing alone.

"And for the pivotal role of Thomas Edison," he concluded, "I've chosen Francine."

"Me?" Francine looked shocked.

Her classmates cheered.

"All right!" "Congratulations!" "Way to go!"

Francine still looked stunned. "I'm the star?" She stepped out in front of everyone. "I'm not prepared to give a speech. . . ." Everybody clapped. "But I want you to know I won't let the class down. I'm going to give a hundred and ten percent to this part. You have my promise."

Chapter 3

. . . .

Francine went to the town library right after school. She ran up to the librarian, Ms. Turner, who was looking over some new books.

"Good afternoon, Ms. Turner."

"Hello, Francine. What can I do for you? A good mystery? Action/adventure? Historical fiction?"

Francine shook her head. "Not today. Actually, I'm here on official business. You may have heard that I was given the lead in my class play."

"No, I'm afraid that news hadn't reached us yet."

"Well, it's true. It's a play about Thomas Edison — and I'm playing his part. It's the role of a lifetime. I've read everything in the school library already, but I need to find out more. Can you point me toward the Thomas Edison room?"

Ms. Turner frowned. "Francine, I don't believe we have a Thomas Edison room."

"Oh?" Francine looked surprised. "Okay, then where's the Thomas Edison section?"

"You need to check the biographies. Naturally, you'll find Mr. Edison under *E.*"

Francine looked shocked. "Ms. Turner, are you saying he's just mixed in with all the other people?"

"That's right," said Ms. Turner. "He doesn't have his own section. You'll find him somewhere between Amelia Earhart and Albert Einstein."

Francine did not look happy. "You know, Ms. Turner, I'm not sure the library is showing Mr. Edison the proper respect."

"Oh? What do you mean?"

"Well, he is the greatest inventor our country has ever had. He came up with the electric light — and all the wiring and switches to install it in cities — and the phonograph and the movie camera. If you took all of the things his inventions led to away from this library, it would be a very different place."

"I'm sure that's true," said Ms. Turner.

"Exactly," said Francine. "A person like that should at least have his own section," Francine insisted. "And maybe a statue somewhere up front."

Ms. Turner smiled. "Francine, I'll share your enthusiasm with the library trustees at the next meeting. Meanwhile, you and Mr. Edison will have to be satisfied with his current location."

A short while later Francine left the library balancing a huge pile of books on her bike.

She passed Arthur and Buster heading the other way.

"Hey, Francine," said Buster, "we're going to the Sugar Bowl. Do you want to come?"

Francine shook her head. "I have no time for candy and childish small talk."

Buster looked surprised. "No time for candy? Are you sick?"

"I'm fine, Buster. I'm just busy."

"I'd be busy, too, if I had all those books," said Arthur. "What's going on?"

"This is everything the library had on Thomas Edison," Francine explained. "I hope it will be enough."

"Enough for what?" asked Buster.

"Enough for me to find out what really made Edison tick. I can't just memorize a few lines and read them on stage. I have to know about Edison from top to bottom, from the inside out. I need motivation."

"Wow." Buster looked impressed. "But

won't that be a lot of extra work?"

"True dedication is not bound by the hands of time," Francine declared.

"Who said that?" asked Arthur.

"I did," said Francine, and she continued on her way.

Chapter 4

* * * * * * * * * * * *

Francine was sprawled across her bed. Scattered around her were several open books.

"Hmmm." She read aloud, " 'Edison lived from 1847 to 1931. He was born in Ohio, the youngest of seven children.' " Francine looked up. "And I think I have problems with just one older sister."

She continued, " 'His first laboratory was in the basement of his house, which was the only place his mother would let him make such a big mess.' "

Francine looked around her room. She wondered if it would qualify as a laboratory, too. Maybe someday a biographer would write about her messes.

"Francine, dinner!" her mother called out.

"Coming!" she said.

As she sat down at the table, she noticed her father putting salt on his food.

"Did you taste that first?" she asked him.

Her father paused. "No, I guess I didn't."

"Aha!" said Francine. "Edison once turned down someone applying for a job because he salted his food without tasting it first. Edison thought it showed that the man jumped to conclusions."

Her father put down the saltshaker. "I'll keep that in mind the next time I'm looking for work."

Francine turned to her mother. "And did you know Edison stopped going to school when he was ten? His mother taught him at home."

"Don't get any ideas," said her mother.

"That's not all," Francine went on. "As a young man, he was one of the fastest telegraph operators in the whole United States."

"Borrring!" muttered her sister, Catherine.

"A lot you know," Francine said.

"Francine," said her father, "I'm glad you're so excited about being in this play. Do you think it will be hard to memorize your part?"

"Nope. By the time I'm done, I'll be Thomas Edison from the top of my head to the tips of my toes."

After dinner, Francine stood in the living room flicking the light on and off.

"Francine, stop that!" said Catherine, who was lying on the couch.

"Stop what?"

"Flicking! I'm trying to read my Shakespeare homework."

Francine laughed. "Shakespeare? You want me to stop for *him*? You can't even mention Shakespeare in the same sentence with *my* guy. How many inventions did Shakespeare come up with? None. Edison patented 1,093 inventions during his lifetime."

"Francine, Shakespeare was a writer. In England."

Francine shrugged. "Don't make excuses for him. He would have invented things if he'd had the talent."

Catherine rolled her eyes.

"Anyway," Francine said, "if I'm going to play Edison convincingly, I need to really experience the full power of his inventions!"

She kept flicking the light on and off.

"Didn't Edison invent anything else?"

Francine stopped flicking for a moment. "Of course. There was the phonograph, the kinetoscope, the storage battery, and the electric pen."

"Maybe you should try experiencing an electric pen for a while. After all, you want to give all the inventions equal time."

Francine brightened. "Good idea! I will as soon as I finish here."

Catherine sighed as the lights continued to go on and off.

Chapter 5

• • • • • • • • • • • •

On Saturday morning, Francine headed downtown to do further research. She passed Binky on the way. He was carrying his baseball glove.

"Hey, Francine, we're playing a game in a few minutes. Want to come?"

"Sorry, I can't. But I'm surprised at you, Binky."

"Me? Why? What did I do?"

"You're going to be a train in the play, right?"

"Uh-huh."

Francine frowned. "Don't you need to practice?"

"Practice being a train?" Now Binky frowned. "I don't think so. I'm already comfortable in the part. *Choo-choo. Choo-choo.* See?"

Francine folded her arms. "Well, you'd better not mess up, that's all I can say."

And without waiting for him to answer, she turned sharply and continued into town.

Francine's first stop was the local antique store, where the manager showed her an old phonograph.

"The first phonographs recorded sounds on tinfoil," he told her. "Later they made grooves on wax cylinders. When the phonograph needle played over the grooves, they reproduced the sound."

"I see," said Francine. "I read that Edison's first recording was of 'Mary Had a Little Lamb.'"

"Could be," said the manager, "but we don't have a copy."

At the camera shop, the owner explained how movie cameras work.

"The camera operates at twenty-four frames per second," she explained. "So when the movie is running, you're actually watching a lot of individual pictures in a very short time. At that speed, though, your eye can't tell the pictures apart. They all seem to run together, creating the impression of motion."

"Ah," said Francine. "Did you know that a former Edison cameraman made one of the first silent films, in 1903? It was called *The Great Train Robbery*."

"Really? That's very interesting."

Inside the hardware store, Francine examined a number of different lightbulbs. Of all Edison's inventions, she thought this one might have changed the least since his own time.

"Hey, Francine!" cried Muffy, running up the aisle with Prunella. "Didn't you hear us? We were calling to you from out-side."

"Do you want to go to the mall?" asked Prunella. "All the stores are having big sales."

"Sales?" said Francine. She held up a 100-watt bulb. "Did you know that Edison experimented with hundreds of things be-fore he found the right material for his in-candescent lamp, which later became the lightbulb?"

"That's nice," said Muffy, "but we're in a hurry. We want to get there before the good stuff is gone. Are you coming?"

"I can't. I'm not done here yet. But you're welcome to stay and study fila-ments with me."

"Francine, snap out of it!" said Muffy. "We're talking about the mall. Stuff to buy, clothes to try on . . . you know — fun!"

Francine frowned. "Hey, don't knock lightbulbs. Without them, you'd have to

shop in the dark." She took a closer look at Muffy's clothes. "Oh, sorry. I guess you already do."

Muffy gasped — and ran out in tears.

"That was pretty mean," said Prunella.

Francine folded her arms. "She insulted the lightbulbs first. Now, if you don't mind, you're keeping me from my work."

She went back to studying the lightbulbs as Prunella stormed out.

Chapter 6

· · · · · · · · · · · ·

At the first rehearsal, the Brain handed out costumes for the play.

"A lot of people worked very hard on these," he said. "If there are any problems, let me know. We can make changes if necessary."

Everyone took the costumes for the parts they'd been assigned and began getting dressed.

As the narrator, Muffy wore a long dress. "This is *not* in fashion," she complained.

"It was in 1890," said the Brain.

"And it itches," she added, "right in the middle of my back."

The Brain shrugged. "Feel free to scratch. Just do it in a historical way."

Binky was twisting his head around in confusion. "I like being a powerful engine," he said, "but what's this thing I'm dragging behind me?"

"That's your caboose," the Brain explained.

"My *what*?"

"The last car in the train."

"Oh, right," said Binky. "I knew that."

"Don't complain, Binky," said Arthur, who was trying to fit the bell of the phonograph over his head. "At least you can see where you're going."

"You'll be fine, Arthur," the Brain reassured him. "Just bend over a little when you walk."

"Exactly," said Francine. She was wearing a long frock coat and droopy bow tie.

32

Clasping her hands behind her back, she walked back and forth making an inspection.

"Straighten those pants. . . . Make sure that stock ticker tape goes right down the middle. . . . Bend over when — no, no, no, no, no!"

Mr. Ratburn came running over. "What's the problem, Francine?"

"Look at Sue Ellen. She's supposed to be a kinetoscope. But look!" She pulled open the side of Sue Ellen's costume, revealing a mesh of gears.

"Those are the proper gears," said Mr. Ratburn. "They even have the right number of teeth."

"True," said Francine, "but what are the teeth supposed to fit into? Sue Ellen's film has no sprocket holes. How can the pull-down claw move the film without the sprocket holes? The audience will laugh at Sue Ellen whenever she comes on stage."

"They will?" said Sue Ellen, turning to Mr. Ratburn. "I don't want people laughing at me."

"Hold on," said Mr. Ratburn. "Francine, you're talking about something inside her costume. The audience will never see it."

Francine did not look convinced. "That's not a good excuse," she insisted. "Attention to detail was an Edison hallmark. Are we honoring his memory or not?"

Mr. Ratburn sighed. "Very well, Mr. Edison. Come with me, Sue Ellen. We'll make some sprocket holes."

Francine finished up her inspection in front of Buster, who stood up straight at attention.

"What are you?" she asked.

"I'm a lightbulb," he said, tapping the clear bubble on his head.

"Actually, they were called incandescent lamps at the time. But I'm talking about *these*!" She poked her fingers at the openings in front of his mouth.

"Those are so he can breathe," said the Brain.

"I understand. But airholes in an incandescent lamp? There's supposed to be a vacuum inside. If there were airholes, Brain, the light wouldn't work."

"Yes, but . . ."

Francine looked him in the face. "First there were *no* holes where there should have been some. And now there *are* holes where there shouldn't be any." Francine glared at the Brain. "Are you trying to ruin this play?"

"Of course not," said the Brain.

"THEN FIX IT!" Francine shouted. She stomped away in a huff.

Chapter 7

● ● ● ● ● ● ● ● ● ● ● ●

The secret meeting at the Sugar Bowl started right after school. Everyone took a last suspicious look around before settling into a seat.

"You're sure this is safe?" squeaked Buster. "Maybe I should act as lookout."

He was sitting closest to the window. The others in the booth were Arthur, Binky, Muffy, Prunella, and the Brain.

"Don't worry," said the Brain. "Francine will be busy for some time with Mr. Ratburn."

Arthur shuddered. "I couldn't believe she corrected him in class today. I mean, who cares if he called the incandescent lamp a lightbulb?"

"Little Miss Perfect, that's who," said Muffy. "Right now she's reviewing Mr. Ratburn's script to make sure there aren't any other mistakes in it."

"She's the *biggest* mistake," said Binky. "All she does is complain. Every time I make my train noises, she says I'm not doing it right. I mean, I want to say *choo-choo, choo-choo*. What's wrong with that? But Francine isn't satisfied. She keeps saying I should go *shhh-shhh, shhh-shhh*."

Prunella nodded. "When I was painting the scenery yesterday, she came by. 'The background's too dark,' she said. 'I need to stand out more.' Then when I lightened it up, she said it was too light. 'Just start over,' she said. 'And keep starting over until you get it right.' " Prunella sighed. "I almost dumped a bucket of paint on her head."

"If you had," said Arthur, "I would have put my phonograph bell on top of it. Then Francine could see what it's like to have to wear it all the time."

"How come you can't just carry it around for rehearsals?" asked Muffy.

Arthur shook his head. "I tried that. Do you know what Francine said? 'Arthur, you must *become* the phonograph. You're a sound machine. Now do what you're told, or I'll uninvent you.'"

"She's way out of control," muttered the Brain. "Edison was a difficult person to work with, but Francine's impossible."

"This is our own fault," said Buster. "We were the ones who asked Mr. Ratburn to give her a good part. We felt sorry for her because her other roles have always been such disasters."

"And now *she's* the disaster," said Muffy.

Everyone nodded.

"She acts like it's *her* show," said Prunella. "The rest of you are just hired help."

"Muffy," said Arthur, "you're her best friend. Can't you talk to her?"

Muffy snorted. "Of course I could talk to her — if I were talking to her at all, which I'm not."

"Francine insulted her clothes," Prunella explained.

"All right, all right," said Arthur. "I'll talk to her. I'm sure I can get her to understand."

"You'd better make it quick," the Brain reminded him. "We have a dress rehearsal for the kindergarten class tomorrow morning."

Arthur nodded. He didn't have a moment to lose.

Chapter 8

● ● ● ● ● ● ● ● ● ● ●

Backstage at the school auditorium, Francine and Sue Ellen peeked out at the waiting audience.

"Look at all those eager faces," said Francine. "They must be very excited. I'll bet they can't wait to have a real theatrical experience."

"But, Francine, they're only in kinder- garten," Sue Ellen reminded her. "I doubt they even —"

"And this could be their first taste of his- tory! We could be inspiring them toward a lifelong quest for —"

"Francine! We have a problem."

The Brain came over with Buster, who was wearing his lightbulb costume. Buster's face was red, and he was dripping with sweat.

Francine took a closer look. "I'll say we do," she agreed. "Buster, stop blushing! You're not a red light. You'll confuse the audience."

"He's not doing it on purpose," the Brain pointed out. "It's hard for him to breathe. He needs airholes."

Francine patted Buster on the back. "No, he doesn't. He knows that would ruin the whole effect. Don't you, Buster?"

Buster frowned. "Can't-really-breathe-very-well," he panted.

"You'll do fine," said Francine. "The show must go on. And Buster, it may interest you to know that Edison said that inventing was one percent inspiration and ninety-nine percent perspiration. So, just think: You're providing perspiration for

the whole cast."

As Francine started to walk away, Arthur stepped in front of her. "Francine, we need to talk."

"Not now, Arthur. Have you forgotten what's happening? The play's about to begin. I'm busy."

"Well, get unbusy. This is important." Arthur took a deep breath. "I called you three times last night, and I know you were home. Your mother said so."

Francine folded her arms. "And she also told you that I was rehearsing my lines. Do you have any idea of the pressure, the responsibility, the — no, of course, you don't. You're only the phonograph."

"Yes, well, even a phonograph has feelings," Arthur reminded her. "Something you seem to have forgotten. Francine, you can't keep doing this. You're treating everyone really badly."

"Oh, Arthur, don't be silly. I'm only setting a high standard. That helps everyone in the long run. Now, if you'll excuse me, I have to —"

Arthur grabbed her by the shoulders. "Look at me, Francine! Read my lips! You have to stop bossing people around. Everyone's really mad at you."

"*Hmmph!* They're just jealous because they don't have my talent. Now step aside."

She walked away, and this time Arthur didn't follow her. He just stood there in shock while the other kids came out from behind the scenery.

"Well, you did give her a chance," said Prunella.

"More than one," gasped Buster.

"That's it!" said Binky. "I'm going to teach her a lesson."

"Me, too," said Muffy.

"Me, three," said the Brain.

Arthur couldn't argue with them, but he had a bad feeling about this.

Chapter 9

● ● ● ● ● ● ● ● ● ● ●

As the play began, Muffy stepped out in front of the curtain to address the audience.

"Good morning," she said. "Welcome to our play about Thomas Edison, the Wizard of Mental Park."

"That's *Menlo* Park, not *Mental* Park," Francine hissed from behind the curtain.

Muffy ignored her. "We hope you enjoy this hysterical presentation," she added, before walking offstage.

"That's *historical*!" Francine hissed again.

The curtain then opened, revealing Francine dressed as Thomas Edison in his lab. She was speaking to several newspaper reporters.

"It's 1877," said Francine, "and I, Thomas Edison, am demonstrating my new invention, the phonograph. It actually reproduces recorded sound."

"We don't believe it!" shouted the reporters.

Francine folded her arms. "Then prepare to be amazed!"

Francine turned to her phonograph, which was slumped to one side, scratching its back.

"Stand up straight!" she whispered, turning the crank and putting the tone arm on the cylinder.

"All operators are busy," said Arthur's voice inside the bell. "We're sorry for any inconvenience this may cause. Please hang up and dial again."

"Arthur, you're a phonograph, not a

telephone," Francine whispered. "Play the music."

But there was no music. "If you are calling from a Touch-Tone phone, press 'one' now."

Francine frowned. Had Arthur lost his mind? This was not in the script.

The audience laughed as the curtain closed on Act I.

The second act began with Francine again facing a room full of reporters.

"It's 1879, and I, Thomas Edison, am ready to demonstrate my incandescent lamp. It is brighter than any candle and works through the wonder of electricity."

"We don't believe it," said the reporters.

"Prepare to be amazed!" said Francine.

She pulled a cloth off of Buster in his lightbulb costume. However, the lightbulb now had a screen door in the front.

"Your lamp features a screen door," said

one of the reporters. "How does it work?"

Francine tried to ignore the question. "Just watch," she said, and pulled the switch to light the bulb.

A jet of water from the bulb squirted into her face.

"Now, how could that have happened?" said the Brain, smiling backstage.

In the final act, Francine stood next to Sue Ellen, the movie camera.

"Now it's time for my kinetoscope to film *The Great Train Robbery*. I expect that this, at least, will go smoothly."

Binky chugged onto the stage pulling several cardboard train cars.

"*Choo-choo! Choo-choo!*" he shouted, ignoring Francine's glare.

Suddenly, some cowboys came up behind him. "We're going to rob this here train," they said.

"No, you're not," said Binky. He raised

his fists, preparing to box with them. "Put 'em up! Put 'em up!" At this point all the inventions danced across the stage in a chorus line. Francine tried to escape to the wings, but she was boxed in. As the curtain closed in from both sides, it caught her in the middle, leaving her facing the audience with a horrified expression.

Chapter 10

● ● ● ● ● ● ● ● ● ● ● ●

After the performance, Francine sat in a corner backstage. She looked miserable.

The other kids were too uncomfortable to approach her. They gathered sheepishly a few feet away.

Mr. Ratburn came backstage. "It looks like we had a few technical difficulties," he said dryly.

The cast members looked down at their shoes.

Mr. Ratburn rubbed his chin. "Can we fix them before the parents' show tonight?"

Muffy looked up. "That's up to Francine," she said.

Francine jumped up from the corner. "Me? What did I do?"

"I'm prepared to step in," said Mr. Ratburn, "but I prefer to see you work things out for yourselves. I'll leave you all to discuss it."

Francine pointed a finger at the others. "You ruined my show," she said, accusingly. "And you're supposed to be my friends."

"It's not *your* show, Francine," Arthur pointed out. "We worked hard, too. The show belongs to all of us. And let's not forget — you're supposed to be our friend, too. Do you think you've been acting like one?"

Francine started to say something, but the words got stuck in her throat.

"We're waiting," said the Brain.

Francine stared at him. "This was my

big chance. . . . After all those horrible experiences . . . I just wanted everything to be perfect."

"*Too* perfect," said Muffy.

"Well, I guess I might have gone a little overboard."

"A little?" said Binky.

Francine looked around. No one was cracking even a small smile.

"Okay, okay. So I'm responsible. I'm dirt. I'm pond scum. I'm . . ."

"Don't overdo it," said Arthur.

"Sorry," said Francine. "But we can still do a good show together, can't we? At least we can if anybody will work with me."

"How are we doing?" Mr. Ratburn called out from the stage.

All the kids cheered.

"That answers my question," he said with a smile.

* * *

That night the performance went perfectly, with everyone playing their roles the way they were written. As the cast came out for a curtain call, Francine stepped forward.

"It took all of us to make this play together. I couldn't have done it alone."

Arthur and the others smiled.

"But they couldn't have done it without me, either," she added. Then she led the cast in a last bow, as applause filled the air.